CAPTAIN
SLAUGHTERBOARD
DROPS ANCHOR

This edition first published in Great Britain by Academy Editions
7 Holland Street, London W.8.
Printed by The Pitman Press, Bath.

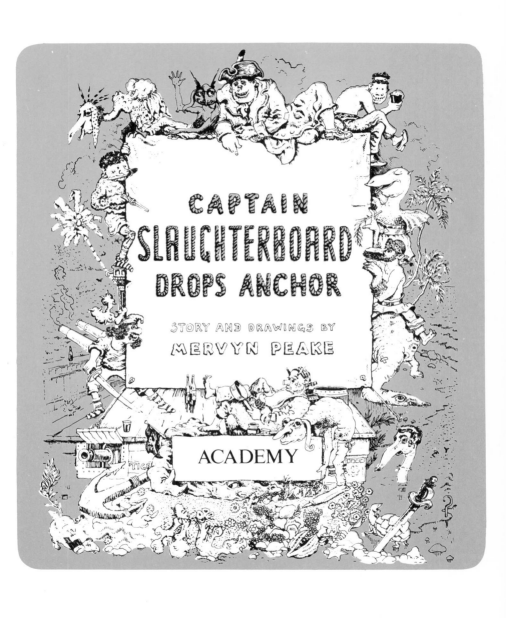

CAPTAIN
SLAUGHTERBOARD
DROPS ANCHOR

STORY AND DRAWINGS BY
MERVYN PEAKE

ACADEMY

Far beyond the jungles and the burning deserts lay the bright blue ocean that stretched forever in all directions. There were little green islands with undiscovered edges, and whales swam around them in this sort of way.

But the most exciting thing was the Pirate
Ship. Her name was the "Black Tiger"
and Captain Slaughterboard
ruled her—every inch!

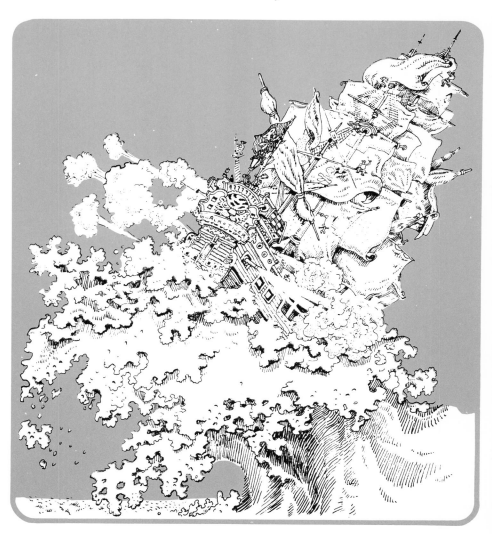

He looked like this.

Lots of his men had been eaten by
sharks or killed in battle, and hundreds
had been made to walk the plank.

Here are the ones who were left.

Billy Bottle, the bos'n,
always knocked the ashes out
of his pipe without bending.

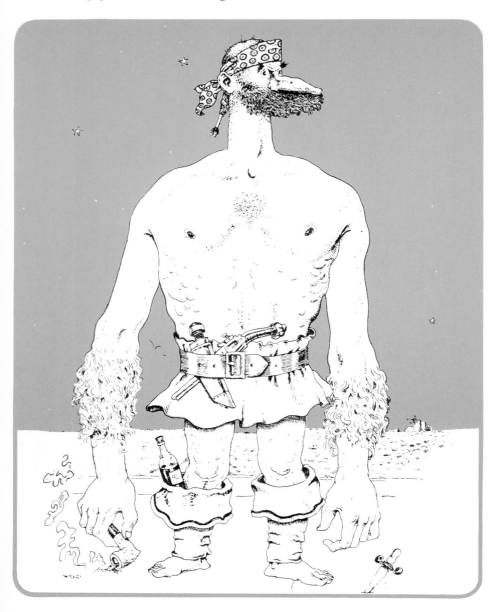

And Jonas Joints,
the first mate,
could do this!

Timothy Twitch was the most elegant in battle,
his left hand especially.

And Charlie Choke was covered all over
with dreadful drawings in blue ink.

Peter Poop was the cook
and he had a cork nose.

Here is Captain Slaughterboard again,
this time pretending to be asleep.

One afternoon while they were sailing over
the warm waves they came across a new island.
"Captain," shouted Charlie Choke, "there's
some land on the horizon." "What colour is it?"
said Captain Slaughterboard, opening one eye.
"Looks kind of pink to me," said Charlie Choke
after a very long time. (He wasn't much good at
colours.) "Pink!" shouted the Captain, leaping to
his feet. "That's just the sort I like. Sail me there
and hurry up or I'll chop you all into mincemeat."

Then he took out his telescope
and this is what he saw.

"Rattle my ribs!" he yelled.
"There are some preposterous creatures over there!
Faster! faster! Sail the ship faster!
I must catch one of them before it gets too dark."

When they were quite near the island
they all jumped into a boat
and pulled hard for the shore.

Captain Slaughterboard sat at the back and
smoked a huge pipe. He didn't row, of course,
but waved his heavy old cutlass about.
"Faster! faster!" he thundered.
"Have your muscles fallen off?"

When the sea looked shallow enough they all jumped
out of the boat with a great splash, but the water came
up to their necks and it felt like a nice warm bath.
But the Captain didn't like having baths, and Billy
Bottle trod on a crimson jellyfish with a horrible squelch.
But they had soon waded to the shore.

"Where are the queer creatures?" cried Captain
Slaughterboard. "Hurry up and find them and
don't forget what I said about cutting you all
up into little pieces!" This made them rather
nervous and they ran here and there all
over the wet sand and up the palm trees.

Suddenly they heard a husky voice.
"Ship ahoy! Captain! Fetch up alongside.
I've sighted one!" It was Billy Bottle
shouting from the jungle, and they
all ran toward him. Sure enough, not
very far away in the green shadows
was a creature as bright as butter.

"Just exactly the sort I've been wanting,"
yelled Captain Slaughterboard as he
charged over the fruit and turtles that
covered the ground. "After him, you dogs!"

Billy Bottle was the swiftest because of his long arms,
and he caught the Yellow Creature just as
he was about to hide in a hollow tree.
"Fetch him aboard the Black Tiger,"
said the Captain when he had stopped panting.
"Careful . . . careful . . ."

Peter Poop and Jonas Joints walked on each side
of the little Yellow Creature and held his hands.
But the Yellow Creature didn't really
want to escape because he had been
rather lonely on the island. You see, nearly all
the other creatures were purple.

There was the Balleroon
with his backbone
made out of three-ply
(that means
very thin
wood) . . .

And the Dignipomp . . .

And the Hunchabil
whose dreadful croaking
always got on the Yellow
Creature's nerves . . .

The lonely Mousterashe
who was sensitive
and didn't make
friends very
easily . . .

And the Guggaflop who
was very, very lazy . . .

Saggerdroop with his
melancholy eyes
as rich as topaz . . .
Not to speak of the two
loathsome Squirmarins.

They all hid in the shadows
of the warm rocks
and watched the Pirates
take the Yellow Creature
away in a boat.

All except the Sleeka and his son who
watched it all happening with their
heads sticking out of the smooth sea.

And the Plummet who lived in a deep
world under the waves, among the
starfish and the sponges, the fishes and
the pearls. He couldn't *see* that anything
was happening but he *felt* it was.

Soon—they were on
board again and
the Captain gave
the Yellow Creature
a cabin to himself,
and was furious when
Timothy Twitch
pulled his ears
for fun. The Pirates
were very puzzled
and couldn't understand
it at all because
Captain Slaughterboard
was a wicked sort of
man and had never
been pleasant to
strangers before.

Poor Timothy didn't
know what to think.

Every morning the Yellow Creature was placed
at the front of the ship, where he looked lovely
against the sparkling blue sea. Captain Slaughterboard
would sit upon a barrel of rum and watch

the Yellow Creature for hours on end.
His Pirates had to watch the Yellow Creature too,
but they got rather tired of it sometimes.

Every thirty minutes Peter Poop was made to take the Yellow Creature a tray of nice things to eat. If he was late with it the Captain ground his teeth in a horrible way and made his sword sing through the hot air.

One starry night at twenty-three minutes past twelve,
Captain Slaughterboard felt a bit bored, so he heaved up the
anchor with one jerk, and they sailed away and right over
the horizon, where they met with so many adventures
and such terrible battles that at last the Yellow Creature
and the Captain were the only ones left on board.
They always had their meals together.

Captain Slaughterboard taught
the Yellow Creature some old pirate dances
and they would practise them together
when the moon was full.

One evening as they leaned
upon the railing and threw
some plums and peaches
to a dark speckly fish . . .
"Yellow Creature," said
Captain Slaughterboard.
"Yo-ho," said the
Yellow Creature.
(It was the only expression
that he had learned
from the crew.)
"I feel a bit tired of
battles and things,"
said the Captain.
The Yellow Creature looked
up sympathetically.
"Yo-ho," he said again.
Captain Slaughterboard
walked up and down
the sloping deck
seven times
with great strides

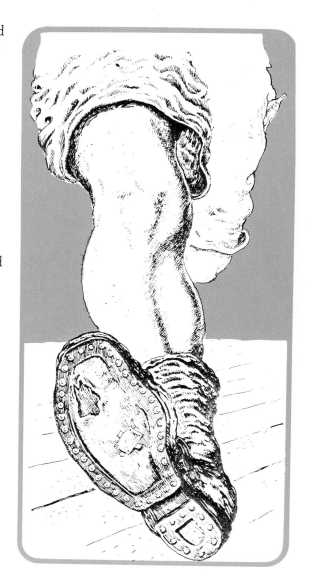

"We'll sail back to that island and explore the jungles
and climb to the tops of the mountains," he said.
The Yellow Creature must have understood
for he got very excited. With Captain Slaughterboard
on the island, he would not be lonely. He danced around
in a wild sort of way, shouting, "Yo-ho! Yo-ho! Yo-ho!"

So they turned the ship around and sailed
as fast as they could back to the island.
Captain Slaughterboard did the steering
and the Yellow Creature saw to the sails.

Lots of whales got in the way but they dodged them
all, and one beautiful bright morning they saw on
the horizon a little pink speck. It was the island again.

They dropped anchor in the clear water when they
were near to the shore. The Captain lowered the
Yellow Creature, his gun and some bottles of rum
into a boat and pulled for the beach. The island
looked so fresh and bright with the trees so
green and the sand so yellow, as though everything
had just been painted, with a big blue mountain
sticking up in the middle like a great claw.

When they had dragged the little boat over the shingle and
on to the hot sand, the Yellow Creature showed Captain
Slaughterboard all the exciting parts of the island.
The waterfalls and the lagoons, the caves in the blue
mountain and the secret tracks
through the jungle.

They met the Guggaflop, who was practically asleep as usual,
but who grunted quite politely when they said,
"How do you do?" Soon they had met
most of the inhabitants,
who were really
very friendly.

After a week or two Captain
Slaughterboard began to wish that
he could live there all his life.
Suddenly one morning he said to
himself, "Well, why shouldn't I?"

He was the only one left out of all his Pirates, after all,
so why should he go sailing around and searching for
battles all by himself? "Ahoy! Yellow Creature!" he called.
"I'm staying here for good!" The Yellow Creature, who
was frantic with joy, shouted "Yo-ho" fifty times.

They are still on the island. The Captain would never dream of leaving and can't understand how he used to enjoy killing people so much. The Yellow Creature does the cooking and can make the most exciting things to eat out of practically nothing.

Captain Slaughterboard used up all his bullets long ago, but
they have both become very good with bows and arrows,
and can hit things a long way off. But most of
the time they are dreadfully lazy
and eat fruit.

Or lie upon the rocks
in the sun, and catch
strange glittering
fishes . . .   like this . . .

like this . . .

or like this.